LYRA'S OXFORD

His Dark Materials by Philip Pullman

NORTHERN LIGHTS

THE SUBTLE KNIFE

THE AMBER SPYGLASS

LYRA'S OXFORD

Philip Pullman

Engravings by John Lawrence

Corgi Books

LYRA'S OXFORD
A CORGI BOOK 978 0 552 55751 1

First published in Great Britain by David Fickling Books,
an imprint of Random House Children's Books
A Random House Group Company

David Fickling Books edition published 2003
Corgi edition published 2007

1 3 5 7 9 10 8 6 4 2

The Random House Group Limited makes every effort to ensure
that the papers used in its books are made from trees that have been
legally sourced from well-managed and credibly certified forests.
Our paper procurement policy can be found at: www.randomhouse.co.uk/paper.htm

Set in 11pt New Baskerville

Corgi Books are published by Random House Children's Books,
61–63 Uxbridge Road, London W5 5SA

www.kidsatrandomhouse.co.uk
www.rbooks.co.uk

Addresses for companies within The Random House Group Limited
can be found at: www.randomhouse.co.uk/offices.htm

THE RANDOM HOUSE GROUP Limited Reg. No. 954009
A CIP catalogue record for this book is available from the British Library.

Printed and bound in Singapore

'… Oxford, where the real and the unreal jostle in the streets; where North Parade is in the south and South Parade is in the north, where Paradise is lost under a pumping station;[1] where the river mists have a solvent and vivifying effect on the stone of the ancient buildings, so that the gargoyles of Magdalen College climb down at night and fight with those from Wykeham, or fish under the bridges, or simply change their expressions overnight; Oxford, where windows open into other worlds …'

Oscar Baedecker, *The Coasts of Bohemia*

[1] The old houses of Paradise Square were demolished in order to make an office block, in fact, not a pumping station. But Baedecker, for all his wayward charm, is a notoriously unreliable guide.

T HIS BOOK *contains a story and several other things. The other things might be connected with the story, or they might not; they might be connected to stories that haven't appeared yet. It's not easy to tell.*

It's easy to imagine how they might have turned up, though. The world is full of things like that: old postcards, theatre programmes, leaflets about bomb-proofing your cellar, greetings cards, photograph albums, holiday brochures, instruction booklets for machine tools, maps, catalogues, railway timetables, menu cards from long-gone cruise liners – all kinds of things that once served a real and useful purpose, but have now become cut adrift from the things and the people they relate to.

They might have come from anywhere. They might have come from other worlds. That scribbled-on map, that publisher's catalogue – they might have been put down absent-mindedly in another universe, and been blown by a chance wind through an open window, to find themselves after many adventures on a market-stall in our world.

All these tattered old bits and pieces have a history and a meaning. A group of them together can seem like the traces left by an ionising particle in a bubble chamber: they draw the line of a path taken by something too mysterious to see. That path is a story, of course. What scientists do when they look at the line of bubbles on the screen is work out the story of the particle that made them: what sort of particle it must have been, and what caused it to move in that way, and how long it was likely to continue.

Dr Mary Malone would have been familiar with that sort of story in the course of her search for dark matter. But it might not have occurred to her, for example, when she sent a postcard to an old friend shortly after arriving in Oxford for the first time, that that card itself would trace part of a story that hadn't yet happened when she wrote it. Perhaps some particles move backwards in time; perhaps the future affects the past in some way we don't understand; or perhaps the universe is simply more aware than we are. There are many things we haven't yet learned how to read.

The story in this book is partly about that very process.

Lyra and the Birds

LYRA didn't often climb out of her bedroom window these days. She had a better way on to the roof of Jordan College: the Porter had given her a key that let her on to the roof of the Lodge Tower. He'd let her have it because he was too old to climb the steps and check the stonework and the lead, as was his duty four times a year; so she made a full report to him, and he passed it to the Bursar, and in exchange she was able to get out on to the roof whenever she wanted.

When she lay down on the lead, she was invisible from everywhere except the sky. A little parapet ran all the way around the square roof, and Pantalaimon often draped his pine-marten form over the mock-battlements on the corner facing south, and dozed while Lyra sat below with her back against the sun-drenched stone, studying the books she'd brought up with her. Sometimes they'd stop and watch the storks that nested on St Michael's Tower, just across Turl Street. Lyra had a plan to tempt them over to Jordan, and she'd even dragged several planks of wood up to the roof and laboriously nailed them together to make a platform, just as they'd done at St Michael's; but it hadn't worked. The storks were loyal to St Michael's, and that was that.

'They wouldn't stay for long if we kept on coming here, anyway,' said Pantalaimon.

'We could tame them. I bet we could. What do they eat?'

'Fish,' he guessed. 'Frogs.'

He was lying on top of the stone parapet, lazily grooming his red-gold fur. Lyra stood up to lean on the stone beside him, her limbs full of warmth, and gazed out towards the south-east, where a dusty dark-green line of trees rose above the spires and rooftops in the early evening air.

She was waiting for the starlings. That year an extraordinary number of them had come to roost in the Botanic Garden, and every evening they would rise out of the trees like smoke, and swirl and swoop and dart through the skies above the city in their thousands.

'Millions,' Pan said.

'Maybe, easily. I don't know who could ever count them ... There they are!'

They didn't seem like individual birds, or even individual dots of black against the blue; it was the flock itself that was the individual. It was like a single piece of cloth, cut in a very complicated way that let it swing through itself and double over and stretch and fold in three dimensions without ever tangling, turning itself inside out and elegantly waving and crossing through and falling and rising and falling again.

'If it was saying something ...' said Lyra.

'Like signalling.'

'No one would know, though. No one could ever understand what it meant.'

'Maybe it means nothing. It just is.'

'Everything means something,' Lyra said

severely. 'We just have to find out how to read it.'

Pantalaimon leapt across a gap in the parapet to the stone in the corner, and stood on his hind legs, balancing with his tail and gazing more intently at the vast swirling flock over the far side of the city.

'What does that mean, then?' he said.

She knew exactly what he was referring to. She was watching it too. Something was jarring or snagging at the smoke-like, flag-like, ceaseless motion of the starlings, as if that miraculous multi-dimensional cloth had found itself unable to get rid of a knot.

'They're attacking something,' Lyra said, shading her eyes.

And coming closer. Lyra could hear them now, too: a high-pitched angry mindless shriek. The bird at the centre of the swirling anger was darting to right and left, now speeding upwards, now dropping almost to the rooftops, and when it was no closer than the spire of the University Church, and before they could even see what kind of bird it was, Lyra and Pan found themselves shaking with surprise. For it wasn't a bird,

although it was bird-shaped;
it was a dæmon. A witch's
dæmon.

'Has anyone else seen it?
Is anyone looking?' said Lyra.

Pan's black eyes swept
every rooftop, every window
in sight, while Lyra leaned
out and looked up and down
the street on one side and
then darted to the other
three sides to look into

Jordan's front quadrangle and along the roof as
well. The citizens of Oxford were going about
their daily business, and a noise of birds in the
sky wasn't interesting enough to disturb them.
Just as well: because a dæmon was instantly
recognisable as what he was, and to see one
without his human would have caused a sensa-
tion, if not an outcry of fear and horror.

'Oh, this way, this way!' Lyra said urgently,
unwilling to shout, but jumping up and waving
both arms; and Pan too was trying to attract the
dæmon's attention, leaping from stone to stone,

flowing across the gaps and spinning around to leap back again.

The birds were closer now, and Lyra could see the dæmon clearly: a dark bird about the size of a thrush, but with long arched wings and a forked tail. Whatever he'd done to anger the starlings, they were possessed by fear and rage, swooping, stabbing, tearing, trying to batter him out of the air.

'This way! Here, here!' Pan cried, and Lyra flung open the trapdoor to give the dæmon a way of escape.

The noise, now that the starlings were nearly overhead, was deafening, and Lyra thought that people below must be looking up to see this war in the sky. And there were so many birds, as thick as flakes in a blizzard of black snow, that Lyra, her arm across her head, lost sight of the dæmon among them.

But Pan had him. As the dæmon-bird dived low towards the tower, Pan stood up on his hind legs, and then leapt up to gather the dæmon in his paws and roll with him over and over towards the trapdoor, and they fell through clumsily as Lyra struck out with her fists to left and right and then tumbled through after the two dæmons, dragging the trapdoor shut behind her.

She crouched on the steps just beneath it, listening to the shrieks and screams outside rapidly lose their urgency. With their provocation out of sight, the starlings soon forgot that they were provoked.

'What now?' whispered Pan, just below her.

These wooden steps led up from a narrow landing, and were closed by a door at the bottom of the flight. Another door on the landing led to the rooms of young Dr Polstead, who was one of the few Scholars capable of climbing all the way up the tower several times a day. Being young, he had all his faculties in working order, and Lyra was sure he must have heard her tumble through and bang the trapdoor shut.

She put her finger to her lips. Pantalaimon, staring up in the near-dark, saw and turned his head to listen. There was a faint patch of a lighter colour on the step next to him, and as Lyra's eyes adjusted she made out the shape of the dæmon and the V-shaped patch of white feathers on his rump.

Silence. Lyra whispered down:

'Sir, we must keep you hidden. I have a canvas bag – if that would be all right – I could carry you to our room ...'

'Yes,' came the answering whisper from below.

Lyra pressed her ear to the trapdoor, and, hearing no more tumult, opened it carefully and then darted out to retrieve her bag and the books she'd been studying. The starlings had left evidence of their last meals on the covers of both books, and Lyra made a face as she thought about explaining it to the Librarian of St Sophia's. She picked the books up gingerly and took them and the bag down through the trapdoor, to hear Pan whispering, 'Sssh ...'

Voices beyond the lower door: two men leaving Dr Polstead's room. Visitors – the university term hadn't begun, and he wouldn't be holding tutorials yet.

Lyra held open her bag. The strange dæmon hesitated. He was a witch's dæmon, and he was used to the wide Arctic skies. The narrow canvas darkness was frightening to him.

'Sir, it will only be for five minutes,' she whispered. 'We can't let anyone else see you.'

'You are Lyra Silvertongue?'

'Yes, I am.'

'Very well,' he said, and delicately stepped into the bag that Lyra held open for him.

She picked it up carefully, waiting for the visitors' voices to recede down the stairs. When they'd gone, she stepped over Pan and opened the door quietly. Pan flowed through like dark water, and Lyra set the bag gently over her shoulder and followed, shutting the door behind her.

'Lyra? What's going on?'

The voice from the doorway behind her made her heart leap. Pan, a step ahead, hissed quietly.

'Dr Polstead,' she said, turning. 'Did you hear the birds?'

'Was that what it was? I heard a lot of banging,' he said.

He was stout, ginger-haired, affable; more inclined to be friendly to Lyra than she was to return the feeling. But she was always polite.

'I don't know what was the matter with them. Starlings, from over Magdalen way. They were all going mad. Look!'

She held out her bespattered books. He made a face.

'Better get those cleaned,' he said.

'Well, yes,' she said, 'that's where I was going.'

His dæmon was a cat, as ginger as he was. She purred a greeting from the doorway, and Pan acknowledged her courteously and moved away.

Lyra lived at St Sophia's in term time, but her room in the back quad at Jordan was always there when she wanted to use it. The clock was striking half-past six as she hurried there with her living burden – who was much lighter than her own dæmon, as she intended to tell Pantalaimon later.

As soon as the door had closed behind them, she set down the bag on her desk and let the dæmon out. He was frightened, and not only of the dark.

'I had to keep you out of sight –' she began.

'I understand.
Lyra Silvertongue,
you must guide me
to a house in this
city – I can't find
the house, I don't
know cities –'

'Stop,' she said,
'slow down, wait.
What is your name, and your witch's name?'

'I am Ragi. She is Yelena Pazhets. She sent
me – I must find a man who –'

'Please,' Lyra said, 'please don't speak so
loudly. I'm safe here – this is my home – but people are curious – if they hear another dæmon's
voice in here, it would be hard to explain, and
then you would be in danger.'

The dæmon fluttered anxiously to the windowsill, and then to the back of Lyra's chair, and then
back to the table.

'Yes,' he said. 'I must go to a man in this city.
Your name is known to us – we heard that you
could help. I am frightened this far south, and
under a roof.'

'If I can help, I will. Who is this man? Do you know where he lives?'

'His name is Sebastian Makepeace. He lives in Jericho.'

'Just Jericho? That's all the address you have?'

The dæmon looked bewildered. Lyra didn't press him; to a witch of the far north, a settlement of more than four or five families was almost unimaginably vast and crowded.

'All right,' she said, 'I'll try and find him. But –'

'Now! It's urgent!'

'No. Not now. Tonight, after dark. Can you stay here comfortably? Or would you rather come with us to … to my school, which is where I should be now?'

He flew from the table to the open window and perched on the sill for a moment, and then flew out altogether and circled in the air above the quadrangle. Pantalaimon leapt on to the windowsill to watch for him while Lyra searched through the untidy bookshelves for a map of the city.

'Has he gone?' she said over her shoulder.

'He's coming back.'

The dæmon flew in and beat his wings inwards to slow down and perch on the back of the chair.

'Danger outside and suffocation within,' he said unhappily.

Lyra found the map and turned around.

'Sir,' she said, 'who was it who told you my name?'

'A witch from Lake Enara. She said Serafina Pekkala's clan had a good friend in Oxford. Our clan is allied to hers through the birch-oath.'

'And where is Yelena Pazhets, your witch?'

'She's lying sick beyond the Urals, in our homeland.'

Lyra could feel Pan teeming with questions, and she half-closed her eyes in a flicker that she knew he'd see: don't. Wait. Hush.

'It would be too painful for you to hide in my bag till nightfall,' she said, 'so this is what we'll do. I'll leave this window open for you and you can shelter in here, and fly out whenever you need to. I shall come back at … Can you read the

time in our fashion?'

'Yes. We learned at Trollesund.'

'You can see the clock over the hall from here. At half-past eight I shall be in the street outside the tower where you found us. Fly down and meet us there, and we'll take you to Mr Makepeace.'

'Yes – yes. Thank you.'

They shut the door and hurried down. What she'd said a minute before was true: she should be in school, for dinner at seven was compulsory for all the pupils, and it was already twenty minutes to.

But on the way through the lodge she was struck by a thought, and said to the Porter:

'Mr Shuter, have you got an Oxford directory?'

'Trade, or residential, Miss Lyra?'

'I don't know. Both. One that covers Jericho.'

'What are you looking up?' said the old man, handing her a couple of battered reference books.

The Porter was a friend; he wasn't being nosy.

'Someone called Makepeace,' she said, turning

to the Jericho section of the residential one. 'Is there a firm or a shop called Makepeace that you know of?'

'Not to my knowledge,' he said.

The Porter sat in his small room, and dealt with visitors and enquiries and students through the window that opened into the lodge. Behind him and out of sight was a rack of pigeon-holes for the use of Scholars, and for Lyra too, and as she was running her finger quickly down the list of residents in Jericho she heard a cheery voice from inside.

'Are you after the alchemist, Lyra?'

And Dr Polstead's ginger face leaned out of the Porter's window, beaming at her curiously.

'The alchemist?' she said.

'The only Makepeace I've ever heard of is a chap called Sebastian,' he said, fumbling with some papers. 'Used to be a Scholar of Merton, till he went mad. Don't know how they managed to tell, in that place. He devoted himself to alchemy – in this day and age! Spends his time changing lead into gold, or trying to. You can see him in Bodley, sometimes. Talks to himself –

they have to put him outside, but he goes mildly enough. Dæmon's a black cat. What are you after him for?'

Lyra had found the name: a house in Juxon Street.

'Miss Parker was telling us about when she was a girl,' she said, with a bright, open candour, 'and she said there was a William Makepeace who used to make treacle toffee better than anyone, and I wondered if he was still there somewhere, because I was going to get some for her. I think Miss Parker's the best teacher I ever had,' she went on earnestly, 'and she's so pretty too, she's not just dull like most teachers. Maybe I'll make her some toffee myself …'

There was no such person as Miss Parker, and Dr Polstead had been Lyra's unwilling teacher himself for a difficult six weeks, two or three years before.

'Jolly good idea,' he said. 'Treacle toffee. Mmm.'

'Thank you, Mr Shuter,' said Lyra, and she laid the books on the shelf before darting out into Turl Street, with Pan at her heels, and made for the Parks and St Sophia's.

Fifteen minutes later, breathless, she sat down to dinner in the hall, trying to keep her grubby hands from view. It was the way in that college not to use the high table every day; instead, the Scholars were encouraged to sit among the students, and the teachers and older pupils from the school, of whom Lyra was one, did the same. It was a point of good manners not to sit with a clique of the same friends all the time, and it meant that conversation at dinner had to be open and general rather than close and gossipy.

Tonight Lyra found herself sitting between an elderly Scholar, a historian called Miss Greenwood, and a girl at the head of the school, four years older than Lyra was. As they ate their minced lamb and boiled potatoes, Lyra said:

'Miss Greenwood, when did they stop doing alchemy?'

'They? Which they, Lyra?'

'The people who … I suppose the people who think about things. It used to be part of experimental theology, didn't it?'

'That's right. And in fact the alchemists made many discoveries, about the action of acids and so on. But they had a basic idea about the universe that didn't hold up, and when a better one came along, the structure that kept their ideas in place just fell apart. The people who think about things, as you call them, discovered that chemistry had a stronger and more coherent conceptual framework. It explained things, you see, more fully, more accurately.'

'But when?'

'I don't think there've been any serious alchemists for two hundred and fifty years. Apart from the famous Oxford alchemist.'

'Who was that?'

'I forget his name. Irony – why do I say that? ... He's still alive – an eccentric ex-scholar. You find people like that on the fringes of scholarship – genuinely brilliant, sometimes – but cracked, you know, possessed by some crazy idea that has no basis in reality, but which seems to them to hold the key to understanding the whole cosmos. I've seen it more than once – tragic, really.'

Miss Greenwood's dæmon, a marmoset, said from the back of her chair:

'Makepeace. That was his name.'

'Of course! I knew it was ironic.'

'Why?' said Lyra.

'Because he was said to be very violent. There was a court case – manslaughter, I think – he got off, as far as I remember. Years ago. But I mustn't gossip.'

'Lyra,' said the girl on her left, 'would you like to come to the Musical Society this evening? There's a recital by Michael Coke – you know, the flautist …'

Lyra didn't know. 'Oh, Ruth, I wish I could,' she said. 'But I'm so behind with my Latin – I really must do some work.'

The older girl nodded glumly. Small audience expected, thought Lyra, and felt sorry; but there was nothing for it.

At half-past eight she and Pan moved out of the shadow of the Radcliffe Camera's great dome and slipped into the narrow alley, over-hung with chestnut trees, that separated Jordan College from Brasenose. It wasn't hard to get out of St Sophia's School, but those girls who did were severely punished, and Lyra had no wish to get caught. But she was wearing dark clothes and she could run fast, and she and Pan, with their witch-like power of separation, had managed to mislead pursuers before now.

They looked both ways where the alley opened into Turl Street, but there were only three or four people in sight. Before they could step out under the gas light, there was a rush of wings, and the dæmon-bird flew down to perch on the tall wooden bollard that closed the alley to traffic.

'Now,' said Lyra, 'I can take you to the house, but then I must go straight back. It'll take about fifteen minutes. I'll walk ahead – you watch and fly after me.'

She made to move away, but the dæmon-bird fluttered up and back, and said with great agitation, 'No – no – you must make sure it's him – please, wait and see him, make sure!'

'Well, we could knock on the door, I suppose,' said Lyra.

'No – you must come in the house with me and make sure – it's important!'

She felt a little quiver from Pan, and stroked him: hush. They turned into Broad Street and then up past the little oratory of St Ann Magdalen, where the Cornmarket met the wide tree-lined avenue of St Giles'. This was the busiest and best-lit part of their journey, and Lyra would have liked to turn left into the maze of little back streets that reached all the way to the alchemist's house; but she and Pan agreed silently that it would be better to stay in St Giles', where the dæmon-bird would have to keep a little distance from them, so that they could talk quietly without his hearing.

'We can't make sure it's him, because we don't know him,' Pan said.

'I thought they might have been lovers, him

and the witch. But I don't know what a witch would see in a fusty old alchemist … though maybe if he was a manslaughterer?'

'I never heard of that birch-oath, either.'

'That doesn't mean there isn't one. There's a lot of witch-stuff we'll never know.'

They were going past the Grey Friars' Oratory, and through the window there came the sound of a choir singing the responses to an evening rite.

Lyra said quietly, 'Where is he now?'

'In one of the trees further back. Not close.'

'Pan, I don't know if we should –'

There was a hasty clap of wings, and the dæmon-bird skimmed over their heads to land on the low branch of a plane tree just ahead of them. Someone coming out of the little lane to the left gave a startled exclamation and then passed on.

Lyra slowed down and looked into the window of the bookshop on the corner. Pan sprang to her shoulder and whispered, 'Why are we suspicious?'

'I don't know. But we are.'

'It's the alchemy.'

'Would we be less suspicious if he was an ordinary Scholar?'

'Yes. Alchemy's nonsense.'

'But that's a problem for the witch, not for us –'

Behind them the dæmon in the tree uttered a soft rattling sort of cry, followed by a quiet 'Wheee-cha!' The kind of bird he was, the real bird, would make a cry like that. It sounded like a warning. Lyra and Pan understood: he meant move on, we must hurry, we can't stand around. But it had the effect of arousing some pigeons roosting in the tree-tops. They awoke at once and flew down with a clatter of wings, furious, and chased away the dæmon, who darted out into the broad space of St Giles' and shot up high into the night sky. The pigeons gave chase, but not for long; they were less aggressive than the starlings, or else they were simply sleepier. With a lot of grumbling and fussing, they flapped back up to their nest and went to sleep.

'Where did he go?' said Lyra, scanning the sky above St John's College.

'There he is …'

A darker speck than the sky was roving uncertainly back and forth, and then he found them and skimmed low to perch on a windowsill that was barred with an iron grille. Lyra moved towards it casually, and when they were close enough for Pan to do it without alarming the dæmon-bird, he sprang up to the grille beside him. Lyra loved the way he did that: one fluent movement, utterly silent, his balance perfect.

'Is it far now?' said the dæmon shakily.

'Not far,' said Pantalaimon. 'But you haven't told us the whole truth. What are you afraid of?'

The dæmon-bird tried to fly away, but found in the same instant that Pan had his tail firmly in the grasp of one strong paw. Wings flapping hard, the dæmon fell awkwardly against the grating, and cried out in the strange rattling cooing sound that had enraged the pigeons – and almost at once fell silent, in case they heard and attacked again. He struggled back up to the perch.

Lyra was standing as close as she could.

'If you don't tell us the truth, we might lead you into trouble,' she said. 'We can tell this is dangerous, whatever it is. Your witch ought to know that. If she was here, she'd make you tell us the truth, or tell it herself. What are you going to this man for?'

'I have to ask for something,' the dæmon said unhappily, with a wild quiver in his voice.

'What? – and you have to tell us.'

'A medicine for my witch. This man can make an elixir …'

'How does she know that?'

'Dr Lanselius has visited him. He knows. He could vouch for it.'

Dr Lanselius was the consul of all the witch-clans at Trollesund, in the far north. Lyra remembered her visit to his house, and the secret she'd overheard – the secret which had had such momentous consequences. She would have trusted Dr Lanselius; but could she trust what someone else claimed on his behalf? And as for an elixir …

'Why does your witch need a human medicine? Haven't the witches got all kinds of remedies of their own?'

'Not for this sickness. It's a new kind. Only the gold elixir can cure it.'

'If she is sick,' said Pan, 'why are you healthy?'

The bird shrank back into the shadow. A middle-aged couple was passing, arm in arm, their dæmons, a mouse and a squirrel, looking back with curious eyes.

'That is the sickness,' came the shaky words from the shadow. 'It is a new kind, from the south. Witches fade and die, and we dæmons don't die with them. I have known three of our clan-sisters fall sick with it, and their dæmons are still alive – alone and cold …'

Pantalaimon gave a little mew of distress and flowed on to Lyra's shoulder. She put her hand up to hold him firmly.

'Why didn't you say?' she said.

'I was ashamed. I thought you would shun me. The birds can sense it – they know I bring sickness. That's why they attack me. All the way I have had to avoid flocks of birds, flying many leagues out of the way ...'

The poor thing looked so wretched, huddled there in the cold shadow; and the thought of his witch, waiting in the north in the faint hope that he'd bring back something to heal her, made tears come to Lyra's eyes. Pan had told her she was too soft and too warm-hearted, but it was no good telling her about it. Since she and Will had parted two years before, the slightest thing had the power to move her to pity and distress; it felt as if her heart were bruised for ever.

'Then come on,' she said. 'Let's get to Juxon Street. It's not far now.'

She moved on quickly, with Pan leaping ahead. A dozen troubling thoughts were passing over her mind like cloud-shadows swiftly skimming over a cornfield on a breezy day, but there be, in the words of the perhaps not geographically well-informed poet Oscar Baedecker, *'the coastline Oxford shares with Bohemia'*.

Juxon-Street runs from the northern end of Walton-Street west-ward towards the Canal. It consists, in the main, of well-preserved terraces of small and respectable houses in brick. There have been dwellings on this spot for at least a thousand years, and it was in a house in this street that Randolph Lucy, in 1668, established his alchemical laboratory.

Lucy and his eagle-dæmon were a familiar sight in the narrow lanes leading down to the river during the latter part of the seventeenth century. Many were the stories of strange sounds and smells emanating from the cellar in which he vainly tried to turn lead into gold. It was said that he kept a dozen or more spirits captive in glass bottles, and that on still nights his neighbours could hear their faint cries.

Lucy died in 1702, the victim, it was said, of a spell laid by a witch whose love he had spurned. His body was found stretched out in front of his furnace, surrounded by the shattered remains of several glass vessels. On the night of his death, all the birds of Oxford shrieked without pause for several hours, *'with a Tumult and Frenzie the like of which no Man had ever heard before.'*

The precise location of Lucy's house and laboratory are unknown.

The Eagle Ironworks, which now stand behind Juxon-Street, bor-dering the canal, have no connection, as far as is known to the present writer, with the metallurgical experiments of this sinister Bohemian of centuries past. The company was founded by the celebrated ironmaster Walter Thrupp in 1812, partly in order to cast the new *'Thunderer'* cannon designed for use in the Baltic Wars by Her Majesty's Navy. **Port Meadow** (see p.17-19), just across the Oxford Canal, was comman-deered for the testing of this fearsome weapon, which caused great distress and not a little suffering to the market-gardeners of Oseney.

However, for many years now, the Eagle Ironworks has been serving the arts of peace. Manhole-covers, iron railings, lamp-posts and the like are cast in their hundreds of thousands, and carried to all parts of the kingdom by the gaily-painted narrow boats that unload their ore and coal, and take on the finished products, at the busy wharves behind the foundries.

A tour of the Ironworks, with a historical introduction, may be arranged by appointment. Visitors may also see the small museum, which contains one of the original *'Thunderer'* cannons on which the company's fortune was founded.

The Oxford Canal connects the city of Oxford with the great network of canals extending from the Gyptian fastness of Eastern Anglia to the coal-grounds of the West Midlands. For some hundreds of years the canal, and those who lived and worked on it, were regarded with some suspicion by the respectable citizens of Oxford, who nevertheless depended on the canal-boats for the goods and raw materials they brought to the city's shops, markets and factories.

The canal itself is of ancient construction, dating back as far as Roman times. Indeed, a Roman canal-boat was discovered deep under the mud at Isis Lock, and raised by archaeologists, who believe that it was sunk deliberately as a sacrifice to the water-god Fluvius. The skeletons of five children were found in the hold. The boat and all its contents may be seen at the **City Museum** in St Aldate's (p.28).

In the Cold Ages the canal fell into disrepair, and its frozen surface was used as a ski-road by raiding parties of northern barbarians. In 1005 there was a great battle at **Wolvercote** (then known as Ulfgarcote), on the northern edge of Port Meadow, between a raiding party from the Viking kingdom of Jorvik and a band of stout-hearted Oxford citizens, together with their valiant Gyptian allies, at which the raiders were routed and their power broken for good.

This marked the first association between Oxford and the Gyptians. It has continued for nearly a thousand years of unbroken commerce and somewhat wary friendship. The great event in the Gyptian calendar is the annual **Horse Fair** in the second full week of July, during which Port Meadow is bright with flags, banners, tents, and pavilions, and the coloured silks and rosettes of the horses being shown and traded, while the canal itself is crowded from Folly Bridge to Wolvercote with narrow boats from every part of the kingdom. It is said that more small objects vanish from unguarded windowsills during the week of the Horse Fair than at any other time of year; and it is a remarkable fact that more children are born in Oxford in April than in any other month.

Jericho is also home to the world-famous **Fell Press**, in its grand neo-classical buildings in Great Clarendon Street. This dates from the very beginnings of printing in Oxford, when Joachim Fell, a refugee from the religious persecutions in Mainz, arrived in Oxford with some of the types from Gutenberg's famous press. The whole history of Oxford as a centre of printing and publishing is well told in R. Heapy's *Five Centuries of Printing in Oxford* (Fell Press, 20 guineas).

It is said that the buildings of the Press were erected on the foundations of a Roman temple of Mithras, and that the early printers were greatly troubled by night-ghasts. In the early seventeenth century, one Lolly Parsons, a notorious woman of easy virtue, operated a tavern in the very press itself during the hours of darkness, unknown to the pious owners. It was said to be very popular with the Scholars of Worcester and the gyptian boatmen. A plague-pit on the southern side of the main building was accidentally opened during the course of repairs and extensions in the eighteenth century, and the noxious emanations made the entire district uninhabitable for weeks.

Relations between the Fell Press and the University have been close, but stormy. At one point it was proposed to incorporate the Press as a college, and some elderly or impressionable editors, it is said, never recovered from the disappointment of learning that this was forbidden by ancient statute. Today the Press is a busy commercial and academic publishing house, an ornament to Jericho and to the city as a whole.

The Oratory of St Barnabas the Chymist, the work of Sir Arthur Blomfield, towers over the back-streets of Jericho, and is a familiar landmark visible from as far away as the woods of White Ham. A striking building, it was designed in the Venetian style, and dedicated to the lesser St Barnabas, a saint otherwise little celebrated.

It is said that St Barnabas was an early experimental theologian living in Palmyra during the latter part of the 3rd century. He invented an apparatus for the purification of certain rare essences and fragrant oils, and became perfumer-in-chief to Queen Zenobia. He was beheaded wasn't time to hold them back and examine them, because already they were turning down Little Clarendon Street, that row of fashionable dress shops and chic cafés, where the gilded youth of Lyra's Oxford passed the time; and then right into Walton Street, with the great classical bulk of the Fell Press on the left. They were in Jericho now.

Juxon Street was one of the little streets of terraced brick houses that ran down to the canal: the homes of labourers, workers at the Press or the Eagle Ironworks behind the street, watermen and their families. Beyond the canal, the open expanse of Port Meadow stretched almost as far as the hills and woods of White Ham, and Lyra could hear the cry of some night bird out on the distant river.

At the corner of the street Pantalaimon waited for Lyra to come close, and leapt to her shoulder again.

'Where is he?' she whispered.

'In the elm tree just back there. He's watching. How far down is the house?'

Lyra looked at the numbers on the doors

of the nearest houses.

'Must be the other end,' she said. 'Near the canal …'

The other end of the street, as they approached it, was almost completely dark. The nearest street lamp was some way back; only a faint gleam came from curtained windows, and the gibbous moon was bright enough to throw a shadow on the pavement.

There were no trees in the street, and Lyra hoped that the dæmon-bird could find enough darkness on the rooftops. Pan whispered, 'He's moving along the edge of the roofs, next to the gutter.'

'Look,' said Lyra, 'that's the alchemist's house.'

They were almost at the door – a front door just like all the others, opening on to a minute patch of dusty grass behind a low wall, with one dark curtained window beside it and two more upstairs; but this house had a basement. At the foot of the front wall a dim light leaked out into the untidy, overgrown little patch of garden, and although the glass was too dirty to see much through, Lyra and Pan could see the red flare of an open fire.

Pan leapt down and peered through the glass, keeping to one side so as to be seen as little as possible. The dæmon-bird, at that moment, was directly above on the roof-tiles, and couldn't see the pavement below, so he didn't notice when Pan turned and leapt up to Lyra's shoulder and whispered urgently:

'There's a witch in there! There's a furnace and a lot of instruments, and I think there's a man lying down – maybe dead – and there's a witch …'

Something was wrong. All Lyra's suspicions flared up like a naphtha lamp sprinkled with spirits of wine.

What should they do?

Without hurrying or hesitating, Lyra stepped off the pavement and made to cross the street, walking towards the last house on the other side as if that had been the destination all the time.

The dæmon-bird on the roof behind them uttered that low strangled rattle, but louder this time, and launched himself down to fly at Lyra's head. She heard and turned, and he flew around her urgently, saying:

'Where? Where are you going? Why are you crossing the street?'

She crouched, making him fly low, and that let Pantalaimon fling himself from her shoulder as she rose again quickly, taking impetus from her movement and leaving a deep scratch in the skin of her shoulder as he did; but their aim was good, and he seized the dæmon-bird in the air, and bore him to the ground in a tangle of squawking, screaming, scratching anger –

– and from the house behind them came a high wild scream: the voice of a witch.

Lyra spun around to face her. Pan had the advantage of weight and power over the other dæmon, but it would be quite different with the witch herself, an adult to Lyra's youth, and one used to fighting and ready to kill, besides. What did it mean? Lyra's mind was whirling. They'd nearly walked into a trap – and now Lyra, weaponless, would have to fight to stay alive. She thought, 'Will – Will – be like Will –'

It was all happening too quickly. The witch hurtled out of the door, half-falling, stumbling, knife in hand, her face contorted and her eyes bulging and fixed on Lyra. The two dæmons were still struggling, snarling, snapping, biting, tearing, and each of their people felt every blow and every scratch. Lyra moved into the centre of the little street, and backed away towards the edge of the canal, thinking that if she could get the witch to charge towards her –

The witch's face was scarcely human any more: it was a mask of madness and hatred, so forceful that Lyra quailed to see it. But she kept the image of Will firm in her mind: what would he do? He'd be still, he'd wait for an opening, he'd make sure of his footing, he'd be perfectly balanced; and she was ready, as the witch rushed at her, to meet her force with all the courage she could summon.

But then the strangest thing happened, in a second or less. There came a dizzying blow to Lyra's head, and she staggered aside as a vast white shape hurtled past from behind her, straight at the witch. The air was filled with a

monstrous rapid creaking
of gigantic wingbeats
– and then before
she could catch
her balance,
the witch was
smashed back
and down against the
road by the full force of a
swan, flying full tilt.

Pan cried out, for the dæmon-
bird was loose and twitching in his
grasp. The witch, still just alive, was crawling
towards Lyra, crawling like a broken lizard, and
there were sparks around her – real sparks – as
her knife grated on the stone. Beyond her, the
swan lay stunned, his great wings spread out
helplessly. Lyra was too sick and dizzy from the
blow to do more than push herself up feebly
and try to marshal her thoughts – but then Pan
said shakily:

'He's dead. They're dead, Lyra.'

The witch's eyes still bulged and glared,
fixed on Lyra, and the muscles of her arms still

held her top half rigidly up from the ground; but her back was broken, and there was no life in her expression. Suddenly the muscles gave way, and she flopped to the ground like a rag.

The swan was moving – hauling himself along, unable to stand; and just above, Lyra heard that powerful creak once more, and felt the rush of air, as three more swans flew across the canal and low along the street, over their stricken brother. People in the houses nearby must have heard all this – there must be faces at the windows, doors opening – but Lyra couldn't be afraid of that. She forced herself to her feet and ran to the fallen swan, who was beating his wings awkwardly and scrabbling for purchase on the smooth road.

Ignoring her fear of the stabbing beak, she knelt down and put her arms under the hefty bulk of him and tried to lift. Oh, it was so awkward, and he was full of fear as well, beating and struggling, but then she found the best angle and he came up cleanly in her arms. Stumbling, clumsy, slow, trying not to step on his trailing, sweeping wings, she carried the swan to the end of the street, where the black water of the canal gleamed beyond the pavement.

Over her head, returning, the other swans came past so low that Lyra felt the snap of feathers in her hair and felt the sound they made in her very bones; and then she was at the edge of the water and she bent down, trembling with the weight of him, and he slid heavily out of her grasp and into the dark water with a splash. After a moment he swung upright, and shook his wings, standing up in the water to beat them hard and wide, and then he sank down again and paddled away. Further along the canal, the other swans skimmed down on to the water one after the other, and swam towards him, faint white patches in the dark.

Lyra felt a hand on her shoulder. She was too shaken already to be further startled; she merely turned, to see a man in his sixties, with a dazed and ravaged face and scarred, sooty hands. His black cat dæmon was close in conversation with Pan, at their feet.

'This way,' he said quietly, 'and you won't be caught up in anyone's curiosity. Now she's dead, the street will begin to wake up.'

He led the way along the canal path to the right, towards the ironworks, and slipped through a narrow gate in the wall. The faint moonlight was enough to show Lyra a passage between the wall and the high brick side of the building. With Pan on her shoulder, whispering, 'It's safe – we're safe with him,' she followed the man along and around a corner into a bleak little courtyard, where he lifted a trapdoor.

'This takes us into my cellar, and then there's a way out farther along. When they find her body there'll be a big fuss. You don't need to be mixed up in that.'

She went down the wooden steps and into a hot, close, sulphurous room lit only by the flames from a great iron furnace in one corner. Benches along each wall were laden with glass beakers and retorts, with crucibles and sets of scales and every kind of apparatus for distilling and condensing and purifying. Everything was thick with dust, and the ceiling was completely black with years of soot.

'You're Mr Makepeace,' Lyra said.

'And you're Lyra Silvertongue.'

He shut the door. Pan was ranging curiously here and there, touching delicately with a nose or a paw, and the black cat calmly leapt up to a chair and licked her paws.

'She was lying,' said Lyra. 'Her dæmon lied to us. Why?'

'Because she wanted to kill you. She wanted to trick you into coming here, and then kill you, and put the blame on me.'

'I thought I could trust witches,' Lyra said, and there was a quiver in her voice that she couldn't prevent. 'I thought …'

'I know. But witches have their own causes and alliances. And some are trustworthy, others are not; why should they be different from us?'

'Yes. I should know that. But why did she want to kill me?'

'I'll tell you. To begin with, we were lovers, she and I, many years ago …'

'I wondered,' Lyra said.

'We had a son, and – you know the way of things among the witches – after his young childhood, he had to leave the north and come to live with me. Well, he grew up, and became a soldier, and he died fighting for Lord Asriel's cause in the late war.'

Lyra's eyes widened.

'His mother blamed me,' Makepeace went on. He was ill, or perhaps he'd been drugged, because he had to hold on to the bench to stay upright, and his deep voice was hoarse and quiet. 'You see, her clan was among those fighting against Asriel, and she thought that in the confusion of battle she might have killed our son herself, because she found his body with one of her own arrows in his heart. She blamed me because I brought him up to cherish the things that Asriel was fighting for, and she blamed you because it was said among the witches that the war was fought over you.'

Lyra shook her head. This was horrible.

'No, no,' she said, 'no, it was nothing to do with me –'

'Oh, it was something to do with you, though you were not to blame. Yelena – the witch – wasn't alone in thinking that. She could have killed you herself, but she wanted to make it seem as if I had done it, and punish me at the same time.'

He stopped to sit down. His face was ashen and his breathing was laboured. Lyra saw a glass and a flask of water, and poured some for him; he took it with a nod of thanks and sipped before going on.

'Her plan was to trick you into coming here and arrange for me to be found drugged beside your body, so that you would be dead and I would be charged with your murder, and disgraced. She took care to induce you to leave a trail, no doubt? People would be able to follow you here?'

Lyra realised, with a little blow to her pride, how simple she'd been. Miss Greenwood and Dr Polstead were not fools; once she was found to be missing, it would take very little time to connect her with the famous Oxford alchemist, and Mr Shuter would remember Jericho and the directory. Oh, how stupid she could be when she was being clever!

She nodded unhappily.

'Don't blame yourself,' said Makepeace. 'She had six hundred years' start on you. As for me, she was unlucky: years of inhaling the fumes in this cellar have given me some immunity to the drug she put in my wine, which is why I managed to wake in time.'

'We nearly fell into her trap,' said Lyra. 'But the swan – where did the swan come from?'

'The swan is a mystery to me.'

'All the birds,' said Pantalaimon, leaping to her shoulder. 'From the beginning! The starlings and then the pigeons – and finally the swan – they were all attacking the dæmon, Lyra –'

'And we tried to save him from them,' she said.

'They were protecting us!' said Pan.

Lyra looked at the alchemist. He nodded.

'But we thought it was just – I don't know – malice,' she said. 'We didn't think it meant anything.'

'Everything has a meaning, if only we could

read it,' he said.

Since that was exactly what she had said to Pan just a few hours before, she could hardly deny it now.

'So what do you think it means?' she said, bewildered.

'It means something about you, and something about the city. You'll find the meaning if you search for it. Now you had better go.'

He stood up painfully, and glanced up at the little window. Lyra could hear excited voices in the street, cries of alarm; someone had found the witch's body.

'You can slip out of the yard at the back of this house,' said Sebastian Makepeace, 'and make your way along beside the ironworks. No one will see you.'

'Thank you,' she said. 'Mr Makepeace, do you really turn lead into gold?'

'No, of course not. No one can do that. But if people think you're foolish enough to try, they don't bother to look at what you're really doing. They leave you in peace.'

'And what are you really doing?'

'Not now. Perhaps another time. You must go.'

He showed them out, and told them how to loosen the gate between the iron- works and the canal path, and then close
it again from outside. On the path they could make their way along to Walton Well Road, and from there it was only ten minutes' walk back to the school, and the open pantry window, and their Latin.

'Thank you,' she said to Mr Makepeace. 'I hope you feel better soon.'

'Goodnight, Lyra,' he said.

Five minutes later, in the University Park, Pan said: 'Listen.'

They stopped. Somewhere in the dark trees, a bird was singing.

'A nightingale?' Lyra guessed, but they didn't know for certain.

'Maybe,' Pan said, 'the meaning – you know …'

'Yeah … As if the birds – and the whole city –'

'Protecting us? Could it be that?'

They stood still. Their city lay quietly around them, and the only voice was the bird's, and they couldn't understand what it said.

'Things don't mean things as simply as that,' Lyra said, uncertainly. 'Do they? Not like mensa means table. They mean all kinds of things, mixed up.'

'But it feels like it,' Pan said. 'It feels as if the whole city's looking after us. So what we feel is part of the meaning, isn't it?'

'Yes! It is. It must be. Not the whole of it, and there's a lot more we don't even know is there, probably … Like all those meanings in the alethiometer, the ones we have to go deep down to find. Things you never suspect. But that's part of it, no question.'

The city, their city – *belonging* was one of the meanings of that, and *protection*, and *home*.

Very shortly afterwards, as they climbed in through the pantry window with the loose latch, they found the remains of an apple pie on the marble worktop.

'We must be lucky, Pan,' Lyra said, as they carried it upstairs. 'See, that's another thing it means.'

And before they went to bed, they put the crumbs out on the windowsill, for the birds.

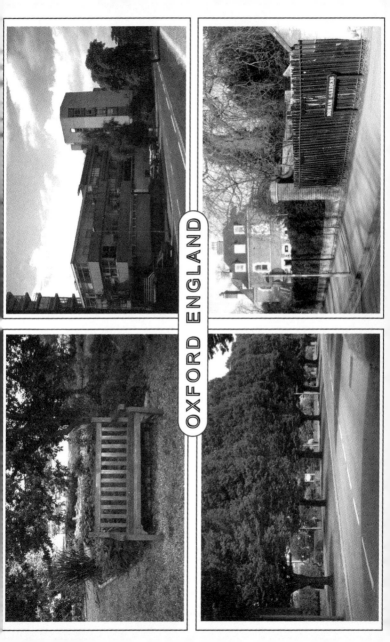

OXFORD ENGLAND

Dear Angels ~ just arrived
in Oxford ~ so strange not
to be 'Sister' any more!
I thought you'd like this
postcard ~ such a beautiful
city, and they produce a
card like this! But it does
grow the place I work in and
a house just around the
corner from my flat ~ That's
something anyway
Lots of love ~ Mary

Angela Bolman
5 Leonard's Road
Lancaster
England

Images of Oxford
Botanic Garden, University Science Buildings,
Hornbeam trees in Sunderland Avenue, Houses in Norham Gardens.

CRUISE
BY

S.S. ZENOBIA

to

THE
LEVANT

A world of romance and sunshine...

OF silks and perfumes, of carpets and sweetmeats, of damascened swords, of the glint of beautiful eyes beneath the star-filled sky...

OF swaying palms and camel trains, of lost and fabled cities 'mid the ever-shifting sands...

OF mysterious souks and bazaars, where the jasmine-laden fragrance of the night drifts out to the plangent melody of flute and guitar...

OF tumbled ruins whispering the secrets of ages past, where the timeless beauty of golden sun on stone recalls deeds of valour and tales of love!

SAIL IN S.S. ZENOBIA, THE MOST UP-TO-DATE AND COMFORTABLE CRUISE LINER AFLOAT, FOR 36 DAYS OF LUXURY, FASCINATION AND WONDER ON THE SEAS WHERE LEGENDS WERE BORN.

Enjoy the delicious cuisine, dance to the romantic music of Carlo Pomerini and his Salon Serenade Orchestra, thrill to the whisper of moonlight on the tranquil waters of the Mediterranean!

An Imperial Orient Levantine Cruise is the gateway to a world of loveliness.